TRUCKS

by Anne Rockwell

E. P. Dutton • New York

Copyright © 1984 by Anne Rockwell

All rights reserved.

Published in the United States by E. P. Dutton, Inc.,
2 Park Avenue, New York, N.Y. 10016

Published simultaneously in Canada by
Fitzhenry & Whiteside Limited, Toronto

Editor: Ann Durell   Designer: Isabel Warren-Lynch

Printed in Hong Kong by South China Printing Co.
10 9 8 7 6 5 4 3 2 1   COBE   First Edition

Library of Congress Cataloging in Publication Data
Rockwell, Anne F.
  Trucks.

   Summary: Introduces a variety of trucks and
their purposes. Includes moving vans, tow trucks,
bookmobiles, and campers.
   1. Trucks—Juvenile literature.   [1. Trucks]
I. Title.
TL230.R64   1984   629.2′24   84-1556
ISBN 0-525-44147-6

There are toy trucks

and real trucks. Real trucks take
things from place to place.

Moving vans are big trucks
that move our furniture.

Long flatbeds carry steel girders
to build new buildings.

Delivery trucks bring flowers from the florist.

Tow trucks tow away cars.

Ding! Ding!
What kind of truck has a bell that rings?

The bookmobile brings books for us to read.

Refrigerator trucks bring meat to the store.

Pickup trucks bring Halloween pumpkins
from the farms.

Dump trucks dump.

Garbage trucks take away our garbage.

Snowplows plow away snow.

Here come the fire trucks, red and clanging,
racing to put out a fire.

This truck is full of water
to wash our streets.

A utility truck brings workers and tools
to fix the power lines.

Campers are trucks to live in.

We have a camper.

We live in it when we visit places
that are far away.